CW01507707

BYWAYS

Edited by
Cherry Potts

ARACHNE PRESS

First published in UK 2024 by Arachne Press Limited
100 Grierson Road, London SE23 1NX
www.arachnepress.com
© Arachne Press 2024
ISBNs
Print 978-1-913665-87-6
eBook 978-1-913665-88-3

Thanks to Muireann Grealy, Sian Northey and Siôn Aled for their proofing.

Printed on woodfree paper in the UK

Acknowledgements

A Drink of Silence © Gloria Heffernan 2024

A Good Day © Eabhan Ní Shuileabháin 2024

A Summer Walk on the Ridgeway © Annemarie Cooper 2024

And Your Shoes Are Soaked But Maybe Mine Will Dry If I Lay Them Flat © Josie Levin 2024

Breadcrumbs © Cath Humphris 2024

Breuddwyd y Gilffordd/ The Dream of the Byway © Simon Chandler 2024

Bridle Path © Mab Jones 2024

Cadover Bridge © Jonah Corren 2024

Dangerous Structures © Adele Evershed 2024

Dechrau'r Daith/ The Path is Another Country © Sara Louise Wheeler 2024

Desire Line © Rhys Owain Williams 2024

Dunes © Des Mannay 2024

Eggbox Track © Seth Crook 2024

Fen Walk, Aldreth © Heather Lane 2024

High Bridge © Mitzi Dorton 2024

Hopewell Mounds © Gregory McGreevy 2024

Line & Squiggle © Marcus Smith 2024

Listen © Maureen Edwards writing as Attalea Rose 2024

Llwybr Cyhoeddus/ Public Footpath © Gwyn Parry 2024

Mapped © Helen Campbell 2024

March First © Amelia Foster 2024

Morning Dip © Thea Smiley 2024

My Home in the Falls © Maddison Price 2024

Offa's Dyke © Nicholas McGaughey 2024

Palimpsest © Diana Powell 2024

Pilgrimage in Fourteen Sections 2.4 km © Sue Burge 2024

Safety Notices © Ros Woolner 2024

Snickets and Ginnels © Michael Shann 2024

Swimming Through Barley © Kelly Davis 2024

Taxila Alley © Raymond Luczak 2024

Terrapins © Em Gray 2024

BYWAYS

Contents

Introduction	Cherry Potts	8
Desire Line	Rhys Owain Williams	9
Line & Squiggle	Marcus Smith	10
Breuddwyd y Gilffordd/ The Dream of the Byway	Simon Chandler	11
A Summer Walk on the Ridgeway	Annemarie Cooper	12
The Tow Path at Carraig Na Siúire	Judith Mikesch-McKenzie	14
Llwybr Cyhoeddus /Public Footpath	Gwyn Parry	16
Snickets and Ginnels	Michael Shann	18
Who Else Walks This Path	Sue Moules	19
Worlds Apart	Laura Besley	20
The Sweet Track	Jane McLaughlin	22
Mapped	Helen Campbell	24
Morning Dip	Thea Smiley	25
Eggbox Track	Seth Crook	26
Breadcrumbs	Cath Humphris	28
Terrapins	Em Gray	30
The Fire Tender's Path	Katie Margaret Hall	31
Where The Ridgeway Runs Into Town	Jeff Phelps	32
Walking with All of It	Angela Arnold	34
Taxila Alley	Raymond Luczak	36
The Haunted Path	Lisa Farrell	37
High Bridge	Mitzi Dorton	41
The turning	Michelle Penn	42
Unbinding	Phil Wood	45

To the Stream	Annie Kissack	46
Bridle Path	Mab Jones	48
The Byway Listens	Lizzie Lovejoy	49
Pilgrimage in Fourteen Sections 2.4 km	Sue Burge	52
Dangerous Structures	Adele Evershed	56
Offa's Dyke	Nicholas McGaughey	58
Swimming Through Barley	Kelly Davis	59
Dunes	Des Mannay	60
Windows 2019	Katie Harrison	62
March First	Amelia Foster	65
Dechrau'r Daith/The Path is Another Country	Sara Louise Wheeler	66
Listen	Attalea Rose	70
A Drink of Silence	Gloria Heffernan	72
Hopewell Mounds	Gregory McGreevy	74
And Your Shoes Are Soaked But Maybe Mine Will Dry If I Lay Them Flat	Josie Levin	76
Fen Walk, Aldreth	Heather Lane	78
Palimpsest	Diana Powell	80
My Home in the Falls	Maddie Price	84
A Good Day	Eabhan Ní Shuileabháin	85
Cadover Bridge	Jonah Corren	86
Safety Notices	Ros Woolner	88

Introduction
Cherry Potts

We are told that Arachne Press has a track record (pun intended) in what academics call psycho-geography: the influence of the (topographical) environment on the thoughts and behaviours of its inhabitants. We didn't know that's what we were doing – we were just looking for themes for anthologies.

Stations was born out of wishing to celebrate the London Overground, because, having complained bitterly throughout the works, we loved it once it was there.

The hook for *A470 Poems for the Road/Cerddi'r Ffordd*, was chosen for its commonality; pretty much anyone who lives in or has visited Wales has driven on and has an opinion of the road that joins and divides the north and south of the country.

We toyed with coasts in *Time and Tide*, which led to a couple of climate concern books, *Tymes goe by Turnes,* (unintentionally – it was what our writers responded with) and *Words from the Brink*.

Byways combines the exploration of routes through our neighbourhoods with those environmental concerns in a self-powered anthology – poems and stories on foot. Environment in both senses.

We asked for rights of way that you can't take a vehicle on – alleys, snickets, ginnels, bridle paths, greenways, the high water line on a beach, mountain passes, desire paths, towpaths – the path to *somewhere else*, the familiar, and the uncertain. Writers responded in poetry, fantasy, archaeology (and in Welsh), and definitely gave us the influence of their environment on thought and behaviour, with a bit of trespassing thrown in.

Desire Line
Rhys Owain Williams

Only after my son is born do I begin to notice how often I chose the diagonal route. The short cut over grass, the slim path between parked cars. Why walk to the distant zebra when you can outrun a front bumper like a gazelle? Now my life is one of slow right angles. Pushing the pram an extra quarter mile to reach a crossroads. Aiming, always, for the tarmac's official bend. The stitches on my shoes thank me each evening, no longer weakened by a daily soak in morning dew. Everyone says to enjoy these years, that life falls away too fast. So here we are, the two of us, racking up hours in extra footfall. Curving the whole half-moon of Swansea Bay without ever setting wheel on sand. Crossing an entire shopping centre just to reach the lift. Every day I look for ways to lengthen the line we travel together. Seek the long road and take it. In the receptive earth we rewrite boundaries, erode my definitions. Reshape the word *desire*.

Line & Squiggle
Marcus Smith

Outside we are sharp corners,
straight lines, xyz axes,
quick about-faces: left to right,
up and down, stop and wait,
go, go now, go fast. This way.

Inside we are lip-biting scorners
of travelling in straight lines,
of following runway time,
chasing railway times,
taking the same direct line.

Walking in the country at night,
taking dipping, curving cut-throughs,
we are stumblers in the dark,
travellers creeping past silences
down illogic's crooked passages.

Choosing a blind way beyond
the streetlamps and paved road,
one last house and barking dog,
we don't know where,
and we don't want to know.

Breuddwyd y Gilffordd
Simon Chandler

Milltir o dir a dorrwyd gan gyllell,
agen gall trwy aelwyd
y brain gris-groesa heb rwyd:
heb y briw, ddaw dim breuddwyd.

The Dream of the Byway

A mile of land, sliced by a knife,
a wily cleft through the hearth
of the crows, a net-less criss-crossing:
with no wound, there comes no dream.

A Summer Walk on the Ridgeway
Annemarie Cooper

At the gate to Fyfield Nature Reserve
there's a notice, Bull In Field.
On a popular track like the Ridgeway?

Through my binocs, yes, not one but two muscle-bound
meat mountains the colour of Cornish ice cream
stand face to face beside a large bush, not a confrontation,
they look relaxed enough, surrounded by black cows

and beige calves. Close to the path though, a few lurches
they could straddle it, hornless but not ball-less
they might decide they must protect their herd.

I take off my red sweater and keep as close
to the field's edge as the wire fence allows.
Whenever I look back the bulls are motionless
each gazing at his mirror self.

A couple pass me as I leave the Reserve,
The woman asks if there's a bull in the field.
Two, I reply

and she looks more pleased than concerned.
It strikes me later that the bulls might add fuel to a fire,
a body of evidence

concerning the footpath,
so now I wonder, should I have explained?

They are Narcissus and his reflection
or else, to be more generous,
twin Buddhas in contemplation
if you keep your distance.

The Tow Path at Carraig na Siúire
Judith Mikesch-McKenzie

The path was a long one, winding with the banks of the river,
pounded flat by years of boatmen's passage. A low mist clung
to the ground and shifted tendrils over the surface of the water.

In the mist, sound and light and touch were one, and the shy light
of morning parted for the soft quick padding of feet
rushing down the hill, panting joyfully. The boy rushes after the

streak-in-the-shape-of-a-dog, laughing, and both plunge into
the water without breaking stride, swimming out into the current
without fear. On this path my grandfather and the grandfather of

the town's famed poet both trod daily, ropes over their shoulders,
pulling boats seven miles upstream to the port while their children
behind them ran and swam with dogs now long gone.

I sat with the poet in his parlour filled with books and papers,
listening to his thoughts on the river, and marvelling at the
difference
in the long generations of the two boatmen who worked this path

shoulder to shoulder. Every stone, every road, every path I've
trod here brings to me the voice of my grandfather and his mother,
the eyes that looked on every challenge with a dare, a firmness of

purpose, a twinkle that spoke of a spirit I found in the faces on this
street generations later, but less so in the parlour where we sat
sipping tea, and talking about rivers. He signs one of his books

and gives it to me as a birthday gift. His wife is kind, glad that
we met in the shops, and she serves us tea and biscuits and goes
to her garden. We talk, listen to the ticking of his clock and I do not

open the pages of the book he's gifted me, but leave it in my pack
as I leave to walk the path our grandfathers shared in years of work,
and to watch a boy and his dog run laughing, plunging into

the river that was once the soul of the town
and where the boatmen worked, day after day
shoulder to shoulder.

Llwybr Cyhoeddus
Gwyn Parry

Lawr llwybr ein cyndadau yr aethom
ar ddiwrnod Awst braf llanw isel
gan wybod bod crancod yn ein disgwyl –
rhai mawr blasus i gyd. Gwyddai fy nhad
pob twll a chornel dan y creigiau llithrig.
Pan nesáu at giât fawreddog y plasty
clywais udo trist cŵn hela tu ôl i wal uchel y berllan.
Agorodd fy nhad y giât a cerdded yn bwrpasol
traws iard goncrit tuag at gae llawn tatws,
gyda gorwel glas y mor yn ein dallu.
Cadw'n agos tu ôl i mi a paid a bod ofn!
Sleifiodd cipar o'r cysgodion gyda gwn –
a dwy ffesant farw yn fwcl llipa ar ei felt.
You again! There is no path!
Llifodd nant fechan chwyslyd lawr fy nghefn
a chuddiais fy wyneb dan gynffon côt fy nhad.
Agorodd ffenest dair llawr uwch ein pennau
a rhuodd Y Major lawr o'r plasty.
Sylwais ar y *shotgun* wrth ei ochr a craith goch ei geg
yn poeri geiriau drwy'i *handlebar moustache.*
Is that you again, Parry? If so, through you go. Don't hang about!
Nodiodd fy nhad mewn ffug ddiolch
ond cadwodd ei gap yn dynn ar ei ben.
Ciliodd y cipar o'r neilltu a'i gynffon rhwng ei goesau.
Reit tu ôl i mi rwan, brysia! Bydd y Major yn gwylio
gyda'r beinociwlars… unrhyw esgus i nadu ni'n ôl flwyddyn nesa.

Public Footpath
Gwyn Parry

We walked down our ancestor's path
on a fine low tide day in August
knowing that crabs were waiting for us –
big tasty ones. My dad knew
every hole and crevice below the slippery rocks.
As we approached the grand gates of the Big House
I heard the sad howling of hunting dogs
behind the high wall of the orchard.
Dad opened the gate and walked purposefully
across the concrete yard towards a field of potatoes,
the sea-blue horizon blinding.
Keep close behind me and don't be afraid!
A gamekeeper stepped out of the shadow –
two dead pheasants, a flaccid buckle on his belt.
You again! There is no path!
A stream of sweat flowed down my back
and I hid my face in my father's coat flaps.
A window opened three floors above our heads
and the Major roared down from the Big House.
I spied a shotgun by his side and the red scar of his mouth
spitting words through his handlebar moustache.
Is that you again, Parry? If so, through you go. Don't hang about!
My father nodded a fake thank you
but kept his flat cap on tight.
The gamekeeper shuffled back to the shadows, tail between his legs.
*Come on now, hurry. Keep right behind me! The Major's binoculars
will be watching... any excuse to not let us back next year.*

Snickets and Ginnels
Michael Shann

Growing up, I lost all interest in books.
I was all for outside, all for margins.

I was poet of snickets and ginnels,
small town adventures, any kind of den.
I loved the hollows within holly bushes.

Once, I ran away from home for hours
after an argument about school.

I cycled to my favourite spot
and sat between hedges in tall sunshine
mulling over the things in my saddle-bag.

Who Else Walks This Path?
Sue Moules

A frosty morning but still bird song,
a flash of something nearly seen
races away into the trees.
A voice echoes in the still air,
arcs of bramble leaves frosted with sheen.

A rumble of leaves as a blackbird
lifts out of foliage, hurls himself into the blue,
a rabbit scutters by. I walk the circuit
the grass folded into this circular route,
one of many who pass this way.

Worlds Apart
Laura Besley

Do you remember when we met in the alley that runs between your house and mine and our mums stood on either side of it, feigning neighbourly hospitality, and I pulled a paper bag of penny sweets out of my pocket and offered you one and you grabbed the glob of remaining Coca-Cola bottles and stuffed them all in your mouth?

And do you remember how the next day we emerged side-by-side from that shady corridor onto pavement sunshine and Cassandra Baker, spotting something new and shiny she could sink her varnish-red talons into, intercepted you and said, 'You don't want to hang out with that skank' and you eyed the length of her and said, 'Don't I?'

And do you remember later that autumn, when the rain fell and the wind whirled, we huddled in puffer jackets over uniforms, somehow staying dry against the wall of my house, eating chocolate digestives I'd snuck out of the biscuit tin?

And do you remember the time we ran all the way back from town, stolen make-up stuffed into our training bras and in the safety of the strip between our houses you said, 'Come on, Fran, hand it over,' and then you whipped out a miniature mirror to apply concealer and powder over the smudges of fun the boy from the year above left on your neck?

And do you remember on one of those dull days between Christmas and New Year we measured the width of the border which separated your estate from mine, heel-to-toe heel-to-toe, and I said, 'Such a small distance, but your world is so much better than mine.' And you said, 'Don't be a fucking ignoramus,' and for a few seconds I hated you and I think you hated me too.

And do you remember that spring day, when the sun clawed its way higher than the day before, invading our territory, you took off your jacket and although I didn't mention that we must have eaten too many biscuits, you said, 'There isn't any kind of make-up to disguise this.'

And do you remember that it was me that cried, not you?

But do you know that your mum, who had never before crossed over the no man's land from her privately bought house to the neighbouring council house, knocked on our door every day for weeks and weeks asking me, begging me, to say where you were or whether you were safe, but you know, *you know,* I told them nothing.

And do you remember you sent me a birthday card that summer when you'd only been gone a few weeks and all you'd written on the back was, *I'll never forget,* and I've always wondered what you meant by that and I've always hoped you meant you'd never forget me. You do remember me, don't you?

The Sweet Track (Somerset Levels)
Jane McLaughlin

They walk with you, the summer people,
heard in the flit of a warbler,
the creak of a trodden rush,
seen in the ripple of spring ditches
shining through birch twigs.

The trackboards lie before you
on the way they built for passage
over rising and falling water,
to the pastures rich in summer for stock,
flooded as the autumn rains fell.

Split oak laid on crossed poles,
leading to huts on higher ground,
the small hill for weathering winter.
Country of winter lakes, winterbournes,
in season full of fish and wildfowl.

You walk with them further into
the low woods of willow and beech
where the light of streams holds
present and past. Where peat
wears away to tell you how

to carry pots of nuts and berries,
to carve and hunt, dig and sow.
A jadeite axe head. Wooden paddles,
a dish, arrow shafts, hazel bows,
throwing axe, yew pins, digging sticks.

Six thousand years.

Mapped
Helen Campbell

Mapmakers have discovered us.
Someone must have informed them.
Our short cut, our private track
now broadcast out to the wide world.

It has many names, our short cut:
back track, metro path, the way
to the shops – depending on
who is talking and their journey.

How did they find us?
The pathway is hidden, cloaked,
not visible from the road.
So maybe the mapmaker walked

here one wintry day. GPS
in hand. Sliding slightly, muddy,
watching light leach from the sky
as the pathway hardens icy.

And now they have captured it.
Counted its length. Imprisoning
its curves, shape, its very soul.
And next will be its naming

and then we're done for – it will pass
from familiar into formal:
no longer ours but something
belonging to maps. Official.

Morning Dip
Thea Smiley

These fields are an inland sea.
Stubble ticks as sun dries the dew,
and sounds like rain.

On the track, I face the wind,
each cool gust a wave
breaking against my skin.

Rooks call like hoarse gulls,
pulling me out towards the trees,
the splash of poplar leaves.

Currents riffle through hedges,
as though the breeze
has lost something.

I kick my legs, past crests
of dry grasses, over troughs –
fissures only a downpour can fill.

Clouds drift high overhead.
Blown like paper boats,
they sail away.

I go home, past pond shadows,
streams of sand and stones,
to another rainless day.

Eggbox Track
Seth Crook

Eggs for sale:
beside a farm gate,
beside a daubed sign.
Please Put Your Money in the Box.

Every Thursday I pull up,
select my half a dozen. Large.
Drop in my cash. Exact.

Until there's little room for coins.
Fresh eggs keep arriving,
No money goes.
Metal climbs on metal.

I start a tower of fifty pences.
I bring a cardboard sign,
Dear crofter, pick up your cash.
But no pick-up.

Eggs keep arriving.
The tower topples.
The board turns soggy,
sags.

One morning: I've had enough.
Time to swing the gate,
follow the ruts.

Nothing much.
I pass a fallen byre full of bracken,
outlines of lazy beds,
no sheep, no cattle, a clan
of pert marsh orchids.

Until I reach a ruined croft house.
No car, no council bin, no caravan.
Only a rusty spud spinner,
the reel still hanging.

So I enter, where the door should be,
see small bags lying about.
Inside: more coins and notes.

Hey, here's your money.
You need to start picking it up, man.
Good eggs, but your box is full.
Dear Sir/Madam, for many weeks...

Draw pouches, canvas sacks,
wren-sided farthings,
embossed envelopes from the 1950s,

threepenny bits, sixpences,
Edwardian pennies,
the ageing faces of Queen Victoria.

Breadcrumbs
Cath Humphris

The irony is, that after four and a half years of solitude, licking wounds, just as we're getting thrown into lockdown, I meet a man who seems trustworthy, who can flip my heart with a glance, and that's all we do, in our virtual space, week after week.

It's good, he says, *this chance to know each other without the complication of chemistry, starting with a courtship.*

A what? I say, longing for his skin.

He sends me clips of old films, in black and white, and says, this is how seduction works.

The actors are immaculately elegant, in beautiful clothes, delivering the kind of sharp, witty one-liners that I only ever think up later. In one scene a man sings to a woman who pretends she isn't interested, but the camera focuses on her foot, tapping the beat. Her dress looks like it has been painted onto her skin. Soon they are dancing, side by side. Almost, but not quite, erotically charged.

This is us, my man says, *keeping one foot on the floor, waiting for the camera to turn away. When the restrictions ease, we will meet outside. I'll set up a camera to capture us, moving at safe distances. This is the new seduction, a renaissance.*

Our hope for a future becomes a day out.

Shared space in the car but no touching, that's the rule. We're both masked. My breath wafts through the minuscule gap between my cheek and nose. I feel it. Should we open a window? Will the rush of air wash away our germs, or circulate them?

The seepage from his mask fogs his glasses. He lifts them off as he drives on, one-handed. *Clean them? Anything will do.* He squints at the ring-road.

There's nowhere to pull over, and nothing in his sterile car. I wipe his lenses with the edge of my shirt. Then hand the glasses back. From his mask to my hand is the same as from his mouth to my skin. We've exchanged DNA, haven't we?

I'm not sure if the ripple I feel is desire or fear. He's in profile, concentrating on the drive, trying to arrange his glasses so that they don't mist up, but not visible, by sight, smell or touch.

Silence. I look out the window and don't recognise where we are, but don't want to admit it. I want to say, *Stop, let me out, I'm not ready for this.* The empty streets were horrible, but worse are the green lanes that have replaced them, closing around us.

He has big hands and his hair has grown long. He has combed it sideways across his forehead, but it's shiny and fine, so it flops across the top of his glasses. The rest of him is clothes, ordinary casual clothes that tell me nothing.

Is this alright?

It improves when he pulls off the road into a car park with pay-and-display machines and lamp-posts that probably have cameras on them, even though we're on the edge of a forest. At one end of it is a building. There are lights on in it, and a few people moving around.

He says, *That's better,* as we get out of the car and take off our masks. We're both smiling, and I think I can recognise his expression. When my heart gives a flip I know why.

We are still not touching when we go to stand by a large map-board and trace a route into the forest. He says that we could buy a map in the shop.

Do we need one? I say. *We could always scatter biscuit crumbs.*

The sky is grey, and there is a breeze. I smell fresh, damp, earthy air as we set off up the path. It's wide enough for us to walk apart, but soon we don't.

Terrapins
Em Gray

Mum showed me where she'd left them
whilst cleaning their tank
that I'd promised to clean and hadn't.

The bowl was where we'd do the counting down for
kick-the-can
so I pictured them darting for the borders
with joy in their bird-seed hearts

whilst I searched for bent blades of grass
as if those small green lockets had the weight
to leave impressions of their own desires.

I tracked Mum too,
followed the crumbs
of damp laundry,
mugs of cold tea
abandoned, I thought, where she'd floundered
in the plains and briars of her days,

not considering she'd found a different path
where she'd place a bowl of terrapins mid-lawn
like an offering to beaks and teeth.

The Fire Tender's Path
Katie Margaret Hall

where winter trees funnel
where munitions once made war

and now we make love instead,
where nuthatches shrill;

next to where bricks were made and moved,
unmade again; and trout dwell in unnatural pools;

where we bramble and ramble and amble;
and two stop for joy while the sun

rests on the fallow ascent;
where twin wheels rose emancipated

from their metal pasture;
where a river runs deep underneath

the hangman's trail
and red shrapnel rained down.

Where The Ridgeway Runs Into Town
Jeff Phelps

On a blue October morning
I meet an old man
sitting on his walking frame.
He tells me it's a lovely day.
I agree it is and when
I ask if he's all right,
my accent setting me apart
as a stranger, a Ridgeway traveller,
he replies *I's just resting,* and smiles,
the sun turning his false teeth translucent.

The woman in pink trainers is going shopping.
She fills the width of the Ridgeway
where it passes between high fences and brambles.
I see her approach from twenty metres,
step back into the road
and wait where it widens, aware
of discretion and suspicion even on
this warm sunny morning.
It takes a while for the ambling woman
to emerge with her shopping trolley
as farmers and tradesmen
must have once trodden this way
taking the same straight track to town.

Now it runs tamed and tarmacked
between the backs of gardens
with overladen apple trees,
burnt-out bonfires and rusty trampolines.
It makes a voyeur of me,
witness to hasty lives,
to dirty curtains, garden furniture
left out in the rain,
green apples never picked.

Walking with All of It
Angela Arnold

Here's one hidden, trodden, nettle circumventing, clipped
bramble skirting, sapling bending, secret
path to buzzard, kite: as was.

Every balancing swerve
embedded in your muscles. Shaping up, slowing
down, whittling away at an ever-evolving thigh and calf
memory – up, over, squeeze, neatest dance
learned over and over each spring through to autumn
return. The catch of mind-free repetition, caught.

Gangs of weather-tantrum trees partner you
like whispers of the sketch-readily still; then storm-
whop you on into a bent-body scramble: brazenly
unsafe, heading for skull crack.
Nothing not here for the in-living:
soft leaf drip and loutish branch poke, implosive samplings
of the best-sunned berries and the irretrievably
soggy, indelibly sour, all the generous plump
of the land and its most peremptory
jacket-snagging – clear enough limits.
Every one of its mood-bound expressions inscribing
its intimate history into yours.

Till the barbed wire goes up,
the yell of a Private sign, and your body cries out: a whole
movingly (dancingly) describable part of it torn away with a snort.
      So? written there in killer letters, nailed,
      metal bold. Sap and blood severed.

Taxila Alley
Raymond Luczak

The cobblestones have forgotten how to hum.
It's nothing but aches.
It hurts here,
and there, and oh all the time.

Much easier back when it was just horse dung and
wheels groaning right back.
The rain stings
and collects into cesspools.

Always better to have shadows huddled in
shroud from sunlight,
awaiting
the moment to dirge again.

The Haunted Path
Lisa Farrell

The vial slipped through my fingers, exploding on the floor. Fizzing liquid ate through the tiles, and a rotten stench filled the air. I flinched, waiting for the blow of the old man's stick.

'Sorry,' I said, but the blow didn't come. Instead, he cracked his staff on the floor behind me, making me jump. I knew then, he had something worse in mind.

'Clean it up!' he commanded. 'Quickly. I have a task for you.'

I knew which powder to use to neutralise the acid, which charm to whisper to clear the air. I was an attentive apprentice, if a clumsy servant. Yet still he gave me the list of ingredients, as though I wouldn't understand.

I recognised the recipe for binding a new apprentice, replacing me.

'Take Rat,' he said. 'Or you'll get lost.'

Rat rarely came with me. Rat's job was to fetch ingredients from the banks of the haunted path, slivers of bone from people buried in ancient times. People whose ghosts the wizard woke by stealing little pieces for his spells.

'I don't need Rat,' I said.

'Take him,' he ordered, pulling the wretched creature from his pocket. He set him on my shoulder, and Rat's tiny claws gripped my flesh through the shirt. Rat was my predecessor, the apprentice who'd disappointed the wizard before me. Rat served as a warning to behave, and a spy in case I didn't.

I took a basket and trowel and obeyed. If I didn't dig up every root and gather every flower on the list, he might turn me into some pet too, or worse. Yet if I did, he'd use these things to bind some other soul to his will, and dispose of me anyway.

'Did he make you do this, Rat?' I asked. 'Did he make you gather what he needed to take your humanity?'

Rat shifted slightly, but didn't so much as squeak in answer. He was a poor companion, yet as I entered the gloom of the forest I thought of a use for him.

'I've an idea,' I said. 'And if you help me, I can turn you back.'

He squeaked then, a shrill and eerie sound under the trees.

'I can,' I said. 'I'm a better student than you were, even he's said so. I know exactly what to do to restore you. All I ask, is that you show me the haunted path.'

He began to tremble, right there on my shoulder. I'd no idea he feared the place that the wizard sent him to. I reached up and lifted him off, though his claws raked my skin, drawing blood.

'Show me the path, then you can go. When I'm done with the wizard, I'll restore you.'

Rat's red, beady eyes regarded me intently for a moment, then he hopped from my hands and set off. I hurried after, hoping he hated the wizard more than he feared him, and wouldn't lead me astray.

I'd heard of the haunted path before I ever set eyes on the wizard. It was whispered of throughout the town, children warned that if an unfamiliar path appeared, to turn and run— even if it seemed to lead towards home. It was no place for mortals; even the wizard didn't visit himself. Yet I was desperate.

At last, the path finally forked. One way was overgrown, with coils of brambles barring the path. The other looked easy and clear, though a veil of white mist hung over the muddy ground.

Rat cocked his head and stared at me.

'Thank you,' I said. 'I'll change you back, I promise.'

He ran between my feet and was gone.

I took the haunted path. With each step, the forest

quietened. The chill mist rose, and I stooped, searching the ground. I did not touch the bones; I took only what was on the list, everything he'd asked for. I nipped buds, tore roots from the earth, all the while muttering: 'I'm taking these to the wizard, who wants to hitch a ride?'

I felt a cold breath on my cheek, a ghostly touch on the back of my neck, but they didn't hurt me. I wouldn't bind them with charms or wards. I offered them a chance to take back what was theirs from the old man.

*

He struck me as I came in the door, and I feared Rat had betrayed me.

'Where's Rat?' he demanded.

'I don't know,' I said. 'He took fright. I'm sure he'll be home soon.'

'Did you get everything?' He snatched the basket from my hands and rifled through the contents, nodding to himself. 'This won't take long,' he said, laying the ingredients out on his workbench.

'What will you do with me?' I asked. 'When you have your new apprentice?'

He snorted. 'Stupid girl, I don't make the charm to bind a new servant. You were trouble enough to train.'

'Then what...?' I began, but he didn't need to answer. I should have known. He intended to bind me again, to tighten his control, to make me more compliant and less myself.

He wouldn't get the chance. As he sliced a root along its length to release the juice, a thin tendril of white mist rose to coil up his arm. He didn't notice, focussed as he was on his work. Until the mist reached his ear, finding its way inside.

He dropped the knife, staggering from the table. I stepped aside and let him fall to the floor, clutching his head.

'What have you done?' he asked, as more spirits seeped

from the roots and flowers that had carried them.

'They've come to take back what you stole,' I said. 'All the old souls you used.'

He gaped as mist filled his mouth and nose and clouded his eyes. Every fragment of bone he'd ground to powder and consumed. He'd gained knowledge, insight, even life from those dead things. Now, they would take it all back.

High Bridge
Mitzi Dorton

Spirits lost to the mines
Hung in the ethers
Laced the mountains
Whispers and siphoned wails echoed
Beside the high bridge

Wary, quick, she ran sometimes
Not afraid of the dead, but
No options if a train came
Someone asked her,
What did your mama say about you crossing that high bridge?

Eyes chinquapin-wide,
Why, she crossed it herself!
Out of countenance, dizzy, remembering the heights
On that bridge, and her mother,
Scarf tight in a knot under the chin carrying a sack of meal
That's how it was in that coal town,
No outs

The Turning
Michelle Penn

They say the body remembers :
                    his body remembering her a step behind
        the single path   that midway point between deepest stillness
                                        and upper air
            yet he couldn't hear
not her feet not her breath   as though she'd already returned
to water
            to the single drop that birthed her

                            *

He'd intended to obey : the *nots* were so strict
                        do not turn   do not seek out
                            her face
                        he held the words close to his chest
                            warm armour   easy music

                            *

The path changing :
                    becoming less underworld and more world
                    he imagining emergence from that mushy dark
                        into spirit and movement
                                    operation and precision
                            day and daily life fused together
                        a steel wedding dress

                            *

The path changing :
                petrifying beneath her feet
        urging her toward the moment they would surface
                        as after a bomb
                climb out through collapsed houses
                                back to ravage and fire
                not even a single field clinging to green

                            *

                    do not turn   not
                        while you still sojourn below

                            *

She followed him
                followed the path   debris rough at her heels
        tang of metal dusting her tongue
                blasts ahead imposing themselves on silence
        ambulances   glass-fracture and cries

                his breath a low hum to calm her perhaps
                                or himself

                            *

43

She could have done anything to make him –

    she could have –
        swallowed a netherworld butterfly
        or sung as though sickness were forcing the tune
    separated herself into voices   distracted him
            with her shattering
      perhaps staged a stumble
        feigned a leg that could carry no weight

           *

She could have done anything to make him –
      but she waited   waited

           *

And the turning:
late darkness
yet she saw it
the light
of his torch
as it bore toward her
      one moment between shoulder and eye
the turning and the knowing
    he'd dug
        to the bottom of a shadow
           to find only himself

Unbinding
Phil Wood

A clinging path, umbilical
twist in mist, disconnected.
The cliffs sneer descent

into a forest whisper
of folk tale, the lichen gleam
on black bark. Best not listen.

A narrowing way, gorse-tight,
a spine spiked with grass. Not on
my treasured map. Then the Ocean.

'Meet me along the fraying lace,
beyond the spindrift of clocks,' she wrote.
No signs. No turns. I wait on sand.

To the Stream
Annie Kissack

I pass at quiet, pack-horse pace
down a single aisle of hawthorn,
wary of strays that go for eyes,
roots that would take your feet.
A hedgerow tunnel dark in stretches,
sometimes gorse-lit,
sometimes treacherous.
Water heard before it's glimpsed
but listen, first, for lesser things:
snap back of briar whip,
wren's fierce flurry in an ivy tangle,
the way a sad gate sings.

Also the shouts of men, unseen,
behind me on the track
who bring their cows down to drink
at a green gash between the parishes
where mountain water rips.
Their speech is a Gaelic not of gods
but hedges, fields and ditch.
To think that further back
they pulled a bronze age axe
out of the bank – a woman using it
for chopping wood in 1900.
Wood from the glen, our straggling glen,
fresh water from the stream.

Beyond the bridge the sun is high,
broad fields swell uninhibited;
there are meadows for the taking.

Bridle Path
Mab Jones

Our horse natures lead us to grass.
Gappy hedges smile as we speed,
gift glimpses of fields beyond, rich
and rippling like duvets. We race

onwards, our bicycles arcing along
a track that's dinosaur-dry but flexes
its spine like a worm, brown and twisty.
We pedal its rises like beetles, hurtle

down its back like birds. Horizon-high,
our heads are halfway between ground
and bough, steady in their stream of
adventure. The sun is a glinting eye.

The fields keep firing their green.
We are getting the thing we need, here,
the scythe of our cycles humming like bees
as the hills beyond prick their ears.

The Byway Listens
Lizzie Lovejoy

Stone Tape Theory, in its simplest form, is the idea that place has memory and the ability to repeat the past in a kind of echo. Projecting sound and, in some cases, images. There are some really interesting ones of Romans marching halfway under the ground because that is where the floor level was for them. But if the past can be recorded by the walls that stand around it, then they could be recording now. It makes me wonder about that feeling you get when you think someone might be watching you… The prickle on the back of your neck, the gnawing urge to turn and catch a glimpse of whoever might be looking. Much of the time, it seems that no one is. Maybe that feeling is simply the big, red circle button getting pushed on the Stone Tape. Maybe it's the future we can sense watching us.

People-watching is a pretty common activity. I often find myself looking. We all get so self-conscious when we know people are going to see us, tugging at our clothes, fixing our hair and straightening our posture. When we don't know, our guard is down, and our behaviour shifts into something more relaxed. Something real. From my seat at the window of the cafe, I see people wandering back and forth through the cut that leads to a closed street. That small byway is sandwiched between the fire station and a very high wall which closes off the route to a different set of houses. Can you imagine all of the things that that place must have seen? And the stories it would tell if it could?

Think about it… It's three a.m. and the hen do gals are wandering home. The group is covered in glitter, sparkling in the street lights, so bright that the moon starts to feel envious at sharing the night with them. That is, until they speak with a volume that could have woken the entire county. The moon forgets its jealousy and starts to wish it could be asleep like everyone else. The byway, disturbed by the sound, starts to pay attention to the group. It stares at their fluffy pink hats, dresses, and feather boas. It relishes their laughter and decides that this happy moment is one worth keeping, the joy of friends right before the joy of marriage. Two different and equally important types of love.

Another afternoon, four o'clock, and the kids have gathered to hang out after school. A blonde girl with hair in a high ponytail, tied with a rainbow scrunchy. It's her piece of defiance against the cold grey school uniform blazer and skirt. She splits off from the group and hides in the cut for a moment, because she'd gained a reputation for toughness that she'd very much like to keep intact. A girl from the North has to keep herself strong, yes it is freezing and no, she will not be wearing a coat under any circumstances. No person can keep that up forever, and tucked away in the safety of this underpopulated alley, she can take a moment to cry. Not choking sobs, mind you, that would smear her perfectly applied foundation, too orange to match her skin tone, and the mascara so thick and clunky that nothing but the biggest waterfall could shift it. She takes a quiet breath, a gasp, shaky and uncertain, with water never fully leaving her eyes before she catches it on her sleeve.

Now it's Saturday afternoon, and two people wander slowly through the byway. Laughter echoes quietly, bouncing between the walls of the fire station and the attached street. They've known one another for months now, but this is the first time they've been out together on something which could be called a date, if either of them had the confidence to say that. One looks at the other, who is glowing with happiness and pauses in the street. *I think you are beautiful.* The byway hears, though all of this is quiet. They stand for a moment looking at each other with a nervous excitement and uncertainty. Breath fogs ahead of the speaker and they pull their scarf up over their mouth, fidgeting, not sure if they regret having spoken. The other reaches up their hand, and the offering is accepted. A shy confession and a soft kiss, neither knowing that the walls bear witness.

The stories these walls could tell… but we can keep our darker moments to ourselves. We can't see the joy they hold secretly either. There is an understanding; the confidentiality of those seen by the street. I pick up my to-go cup of tea and walk, wrapping my tartan scarf around my neck to brace myself against the breeze that floods over the byway. This time, as I wander through, I pause and raise my drink to the bricks and whisper, *Cheers.*

Pilgrimage in Fourteen Sections
2.4 km

Sue Burge

a scourge of gorse & bramble
      I find my hat
lost three days before
      caught on thorns

****

bitter crunch of alexanders
      I want to crawl into this lime-froth
sip its summer wine scent

****

my torso
a rash of hives
      I burn like a witch
          beginning to catch

****

a lamb
races towards
      my proffered hand
bites –
      woolly vampire

****

I know this walk
                        backwards
                        my confused shadow
            snouts for flint & dip
wrong-headed Orpheus

****

piebald
            mud

****

double echo
of two viaducts

*****

Jehovah's Witnesses have hung
            evangelical medallions
                        amongst the cherry tree branches
I don't want to be
                        chosen
      ****

a copper beech
           ablaze
as if the sun has set
       in its branches

****

once I had a stick
       was a three-legged answer
to the Sphinx's riddle

****

a green lane
       deepened by countless footsteps
oaks vault overhead

*****

I lie on the path
tang of dog pee
       tangle
           of goose-grass & violet

****

there is nothing in the sky
       except blue

****

I don't know how to pray
  but hear a hymn of
      goat bells
      blackbird sonata
      lamb chorus
      a cockerel

Dangerous Structures
Adele Evershed

seeing
        the sign nailed to the wood of that thin place
the chapel at the boundary
                        I wobble enough to disturb my ghosts
    they ride by on wild ponies
        in spite and wailing
            'You kill horses don't you?'
                but that was only a song I sang after church
                on Sunday nights
            in our cawl damp kitchen
                the gap a million miles
                        or just one wrong step
                            stepping along Gospel Pass
                    alongside the down at heel sheep
            (daisy bright and relentless as biblical Welsh)
            I'm hushed by the view
        and in the tapping of the rain
    I hear the sprung rhythm of Mam's walking stick again
                        the walk back easy enough
                downhill and lapsing
                    like the priory
                that calls itself a watering hole now
        serving enough Welsh to fill the black eyes
                    of my lichen licked Dad
                he was a tip of a man
                        a Beckett landscape of stumpy trees
            and always boggy underfoot

then growing around my feet I see
meadow saffron
like an incantation to courage
and I remember
this track was always a beating not a doing
the same for all the loathsome pilgrims
and any black sheep looking for a pass
of course the wild ponies have seen it all before
as I look up they pound past
and to my surprise all my ghosts have gone
so maybe now in a minute
I can leave this bloody byway
and follow the path that will take me back
home

Offa's Dyke
Nicholas McGaughey

There were no signs to remember,
nothing to show the way between countries
and no one much about that rich October
bar pheasant, cattle and apples looming

over hedgerows like lanterns.
We tramped past legions of lost sheep,
skirting orchards, churned fields
and damp hamlets, every pub and steeple

asleep under a curfew of mushrooms.
We were giants of the late day
sun, towering over the tumps of a border
that couldn't keep a breeze at bay.

Easy to mist into legend here: rise
a prince robed as an old man,
tottering past the longbows of the red rose
to root under yew trees, wired for the call.

Swimming Through Barley
Kelly Davis

Above Maryport Sea Brows
mind in neutral

I somehow lose myself
in a place I know well.

With no path, I must walk
on uneven ground

risk a twisted ankle
in hidden furrows.

Before I know it
I'm waist-deep in barley

feathery fronds no longer a pleasure,
but sticky, suffocating

A struggling swimmer
in a yellow-green sea

certainty slipping away
like sand beneath my feet.

Dunes
Des Mannay

Outskirts of Porthcawl.
Left past Happy Valley,
on past the Blue Water club.
Down the lane to our left.
Dad helps us climb the gate
that eschews kisses, and we're
there – the Sand Dunes!

There are thousands,
hundreds, OK Dad, at least fifty
paths to the beach from here.
Some steep, for skiing the sand –
stumble and fall as you go.
Nature's adventure playground.
Grasshoppers compete with

the sea. Pond lakes.
Grassy dune mountains
we skid onto the beach.
At the shore, hermit crabs,
awoken by the tide, dig
themselves out. The beach our

desert island. This is where
Dad trained when he was in
the South Wales Borderers.
We find the trench and firing range.
Collect bullets. Green tips blank,
red tips live. Spot charred

sand from target sites, and
Dad recalls what
brought him here. One of two
Grammar school black boys.
Skidding on bigotry, stumbling
and falling – he to the Borderers,
his brother, the Guards. My uncle,

six foot four, was 'too
short' to stand sentry
outside Buckingham Palace –
moved to a different unit. The
powers that be couldn't have
a black man guarding the
royals. Couldn't give that new

Windrush generation ideas
above their station... Dad went
to all the danger zones: Palestine,
Cyprus, Egypt. He couldn't afford to
stumble and fall in the fine sand of
those dunes. Went AWOL in Cyprus.
His dad died, so he came

home. Thrown in 'the Glasshouse' for
his trouble. An older man on a beach,
the sand pouring through the egg timer.
We ski through time so steep, there is no
option but to stumble. Death
decrees the moment we finally fall...

Windows 2019
Katie Harrison

The sun rises over the mountain revealing two huge crevasses which plunge out of view. I imagine myself on its peak, baking in the warm light. I check the time, 12:03. Four hours left. I turn my face back to the mountain, open a packet of Ryvita and spill crumbs over my keyboard.

An email pops up, *URGENT CHANGES PLZ READ*. I ignore it and play a round of Candy Crush. Joylessly swivelling in my chair, I look out across the pigeon-grey cubicles. Each one has an illuminated window and no escape. Scrawled across a whiteboard someone has written, *THINK OUTSIDE THE BOX*.

Stabbing my sad salad repeatedly with the blunt office fork, a reduced-aisle tomato flings itself free from my grasp and splatters out-of-date seeds across the screen. I open my desk drawer to find a packet of wet wipes. After polishing the letters, S O D O F F, I turn to see if the IT department has surfaced from the pub before smearing the screen with small streaks of satisfaction. A queue of high-street suits is forming by the fridge, in turn, they plunge their hands into the midst of rotting chaos to remove identical Tupperware containers. The rancid pong that only a three-week-old-half-tin-of-supermarket-tuna could produce wafts towards my desk, I turn to open a window only to remember there are none.

I swivel back towards the mountain on my computer screen and open Google. The cursor waits. Ticking. I type... *DIRECTIONS TO THE CLOSEST MOUNTAIN*.

69,000 results. I click one. A new window jumps out at me, *LAST MINUTE DEALS TO THE MOUNTAIN. ONLY 2 SPACES LEFT.*

BUY NOW OR MISS OUT. My mouse runs across the screen. In bigger flashing letters are the words, *ONLY 1 SPACE LEFT. 73 OTHER PEOPLE WATCHING THIS DEAL.* Right. This is it. I'm going. Sod this place. I click. Pay and check the time, 12:35. The next train leaves in forty-five minutes.

I grab my bag, Ryvita, and the cheap hand cream I got from my secret Santa three years ago. I ponder my desk plant. So sad. So limp. *You're coming with me,* I whisper. Taking away the only life in the room, I leave. My boss is too busy playing Candy Crush to notice.

At the station, I buy a one-way ticket to the summit. As my desk plant and I wait for our train in the cafe, I see the mountain, this time hanging on a wall. It is illuminated. Biblical. It calls me. *Do you want milk with that, love?*

On the train, I sit at a table and place my desk plant beside me. Nibbling a Ryvita, I put on my headphones and select the *Gladiator* soundtrack. The cinematic strings swirl around me as the drums synchronise with passing trees. Boom, branch. Boom, branch. Boom, branch. I stare through my reflection in the window towards the approaching mountain on the horizon and for a moment, I could swear my plant was waving.

When we alight the train, the wind begins to roar. *Up, up you go,* it whooshes. I don't care that the puffer-clad passers-by are staring through their sunglasses at the girl in the office suit. I turn my face towards the mountain and climb.

I climb until my heels no longer hit hard ground but squidge into marshmallow snow. My plant quivers in delight. Behind us, a trail of Ryvita crumbs marks our path. I tell stories about our new life where there are no screens. No emails. No notifications. I decide I will write invitations to parties. Cook using actual books. Wake up naturally and we will both have sunlight.

When I reach the top, I am almighty. The world is empty except for a group of Chinese tourists. Placing my plant onto the snow, I lunge my heels to the opposite corner of the summit and howl into the air. Nothing can conquer this feeling of freedom, the wires and Wi-Fi of modern living broken free. In abandoned joy, the wind slapping my face, the sun turning me salmon pink, I fumble in my pocket and instinctively reach for my phone. I can't wait to put this on Instagram.

March First
Amelia Foster

The spring ice split this morning,
a sound that calls to youth and following
deer tracks in the snow. But night falls
A half-step too early. My doorway still
holds the crack of my son's voice clinging
to boyhood, calling out as he slipped through
the back this morning, skates in hand.
The fresh milk wholeness of him. He was
returned to me with laces untied,
jacket undone. I nearly reached in to button
him up, to hand him the scarf still hanging
from needles and let the yarn lead us
back through shorn wood. The box
they put him in – hardly larger than a flower bed.

Dechrau'r Daith
Sara Louise Wheeler

Mae'r llyfrau yn lleoli tarddiad y llwybr
yng nghanol y ddinas Rufeinig;

Mae adfeilion yr hen wareiddiad yn sibrwd
Deva Victrix, ac yna Cair Legion,
o oes Teyrnas Powys.
Creiriau fwy cyfoes hefyd –
Mownt Morgan a Pharlwr Pemberton;
fel petai hanes yn mynnu sylw
gan wthio o bob drws a bwa.

Trwy Erddi Tŵr y Dŵr, dros y gamlas,
ac i lawr y ffordd i'r *Cop*; parc chwarae
bach crachlyd, nes cyrraedd yr arwyddbost cyntaf.

Llwybr Arfordirol Glannau Dyfrdwy
dywed, *o Shotton i Gaer*, a
Disgwylir y bydd y gwaith yn cael ei gwblhau
erbyn: Mehefin 2005. Ys gwn i os
wnaethant anghofio, newid yr arwydd
pan newidiodd eu cynlluniau gyda'r gwynt.

Rhywsut, mae hi bob amser yn llwyd a gwyntog yma –
caeau gwag, gwrychoedd noeth, tarmac carpiog, igam-ogam,
di-gynllun. Siambolaidd. Gwyntiad budr, trist a digalon.

Bro fy mebyd, ac mae 'na wir deimlad yma,
o fod ar y ffin, yn y gororau; cyrion, ôl-ddiwydiannol.
Mae'r rhan hon wedi'i hanwybyddu,
heb fawr o ymdrech i'w nodi. Dw'n i'm chwaith, faint o
welliant oedd yn bosib. Ond bysai arwydd newydd, cywir,
wedi bod yn fan cychwyn eithaf da, o leiaf!

Ac yna, ar ôl cyrraedd Saltney, gwelaf yr arwydd
Croeso i Gymru... mae'n fach,
ac wedi ei atodi i ddarn o hen bren, blêr.
Ie, croeso i Gymru, yn wir!

Mae un llyfr yn honni fod *Cerrig Helygain* yn nodi
man cychwyn y llwybr, gyda *bach fwy o seremoni,*
ond y gwir amdani yw, taw dwy garreg,
tua maint 'feini' steddfod sydd,
un bob ochr i'r llwybr cul gwastad.
Does fawr o ddim byd yma,
i'n croesawu, nac i ryfeddu ati.

Tipyn o job yw lleoli'r llwybr,
a digon di-nod yw dechrau'r daith –
sy'n cychwyn mewn gwlad arall.

The Path is Another Country
Sara Louise Wheeler

The books locate the path's origin
in the heart of the Roman city;

Ruins of the old civilization whisper
Deva Victrix, and then Cair Legion,
from the times of Powys Kingdom.
More contemporary relics –
Mount Morgan and Pemberton Parlour;
as if history demands attention
pushing from every arch and door.

Through Water Tower Gardens, over the canal,
and down the road to the *Cop;* through the tatty little
play park, until I reached the first signpost.

Deeside Coastal Path
it says, *from Shotton to Chester*, and
*it is expected that the work will be completed
by: June 2005.* I wonder if
they forgot, to change the sign
when their plans changed with the wind.

Somehow, it's always grey and windy here –
empty fields, bare hedges, ragged tarmac, zig-zagging,
no plan. Shambolic. Foul smelling, sad and depressing.

Land of my childhood, and there is a real feeling,
of being in the borderlands, fringes, post-industrial.
This part has been ignored,
with little effort to identify it. I don't know how much
improvement is possible, but a new, correct signpost,
would be a pretty good starting point.

And then, on reaching Saltney, I see the sign
Welcome to Wales... it's so small,
and attached to a piece of old, splintered wood.
Yes, welcome to Wales, indeed!

One book claims that the *Halkyn Stones* mark
the starting point of the path, with *a little more ceremony*,
but the truth is, there are just two, further on,
about the size of some 'steddfod stones,
one each side of the narrow, flat path.
There is hardly anything here,
to welcome us, or to wonder at.

The beginning of the journey is
somewhat insignificant,
and it's in another country.

Listen
Attalea Rose

I am hidden. Not on purpose.

Start at the mall. Stand outside the vacant store fronts and remember what was, wander toward the soft-plastic play structures caked in decades-old, crusted toddler slobber, sit at a table in the food court and inhale forgotten grease. Exit to the parking lot, through the slowly-going-out-of-business department store. Stare at the cracks in the concrete, the tar used to patch the puckering seams, the grooves in the tar as it settled.

Cross the street. Look both ways. Walk straight, to the neighbourhood pool turned makeshift skate park. Sit. Wait for delinquent youth to arrive, flip you off as they see you, with their tattoos and piercings and lack of helmets. They don't come. Instead, a group of six, with sturdy, well cared for skateboards and hair dyed or helmets in their favourite colours, wave at you or nod. They cheer one another on as they whirl through the old pool, now refinished. One falls, scrapes a knee, pushes the hem of their shorts higher to keep the blood at bay, exposes a swirling tattoo of a lion. It suits them. Another has brought Band-Aids bright with superhero illustrations.

Take a left, toward the woods. Keep walking. Find the lovers' grove, three soaring oak trees triangular to one another, initials of couples, decades past carved into the trunks. E + J. M + B. N + C. A + G. Press fingers against the letters and feel the pulse of the tree, aching with heartbreak for the ones that didn't survive. Remember the initials you carved, but don't touch them.

Keep going. Deeper into the woods. Follow the walking trail beyond the lovers' grove, and when it ends, stop. Stand still. Take a deep breath. Listen to the beating of bird wings in the trees above, watch sunlight glint across trampled grass, breathe in the scent of decaying soil and leaves, spy the murky lake through the tree boughs and the bright-red-with-white-borders caution signs warning swimmers away from cliff jumping, wipe clammy palms against pant legs, recall the path behind you to discern the path ahead.

Two steps forward, if you have an average gait. Adjust lower or higher by instinct. Turn eight-six degrees to the right, then run, if able, or walk. You will stop when you have found me. And then you will turn around.

A Drink of Silence
Gloria Heffernan

When you look at the footsteps
that seem to stop in the middle of nowhere,
you might wonder who
left the narrow trail in the snow.
You might wonder why it stops
midway between the creek
and the solitary cabin
at the foot of the hillside.

I wondered too.
Wondered who had built it
like a lighthouse on the shore
of a vast white ocean.
Wondered if they were at home,
and might offer a cup of tea
if I knocked on the door to say thank you
for reminding me that even here,
I am not alone.
Wondered if the inhabitant
had chosen this remote spot
to welcome the weary
or to avoid intrusion.

I stood still long enough for the snow
to fill in my footsteps,
until the silence gave way
to the gurgling of the creek
swirling below the scrim of ice,
until I could hear the sound of wood
spitting and crackling in the fireplace
even though no curl of smoke
rose from the chimney.

I stood still drinking the silence,
letting it warm and fill me
like the imagined tea,
and when I'd had enough,
I retraced my steps
and walked on.

Hopewell Mounds
Gregory McGreevy

Right time, being the halo
of necessary creeks, being
a breezeless night among
fire scarred brush, where
the grass turned brown,
where the pipes no longer
freeze in the winter, being
the shadows traveling
stretches of dimly lit
freeways, being the sketches
of former humans, being
the realisation that some
dogs will outlive me,
being the bowed trees in
hermetically sealed
communities, where the
mill sits with broken
windows and rusted
scaffolds, where the current
sloshes against lost
footprints in the grey silt,

being the form of continents,
of soil, of flesh, being the
mute thrills of momentary
individuality dressed in
black, where geodynamics
disappear, where Hopewell
mounds adorn walking trails
in planned communities, being
the bridge of continents, being
the bridge of paths cut through
earth and snow, being Meso-American
architecture falling from above,
where the heat falls, where sound
falls, where the ice melts and the
steam falls, being vacuum, being
sound suspended in the ears of
wandering considerations,
fragments of consciousness meted out
in fragile being, being the fog and light.

And Your Shoes Are Soaked But Maybe Mine Will Dry If I Lay Them Flat

Josie Levin

Your hands are wet with effort on top of the last carton
of unbroken eggs, I saw first

we are standing, right now, where you say,
the river used to be and would like to be, again

and you look like you know me, which you don't
and I don't miss (and never have), the water

going from here to Kankakee, which never held
the two of us, together or stroked my face, the way

you say it did, those summers you were young
and wore your underwear into the stream

when you say it wasn't as muddy as I make it
out to be, today

it is not my fault I cannot love, so you say,
the world isn't made for it anymore

and I mean to tell you, when we see each other
again, in the parking lot,

I don't blame you, but myself
it is only polite

and the plastic handles on your grocery bags
seem heavier on your arms than mine are, on mine

Fen Walk, Aldreth
Heather Lane

A thousand trodden years pattern the ground,
scatter the land's memory from Hereward's track
to Giant's Camp; by-ways of place-lore.
Legends spill from the fen edge; from Gun Lane
to Cuckoo Drove – across the Roman Road, to Belsar's Hill
along Aldreth's foot-worn causeway.

Hurdle-rooted, the path's a tree-length
wide, a palimpsest of ancient ingenuity,
driftway, known way, through the mere.
Towards the isle, hunched over dark water,
dragonflies dart above elver-home, where reeds
hush like falling rain. A lone sedge warbler
tills his loss at the damp margin of summer pasture.

Hawthorn and dyer's greenweed grew here when Saxon
harried Norman along the ancient shore, the alder hythe.
Sword blade and rusted chape lie silent in the peat.
Blackcap and yellowhammer flew here
when war cleaved villages and half-built
castles fell among the flag iris.
In the wake of armies, no soldier's name remains.

At High Bridge, only a spit from dry earth, drowned men
echo and larks mock their choking,
smoke-blind from burning sedge. In the fire
and in their flight they sink
and layer the fenland's story. Washland,
witch land; in the cathedral shadow –
heathen land. Where are those giants now?

Palimpsest
Diana Powell

Stone/Cerrig

Stone. Beneath our feet.

Beginnings. 'Bone,' Old Man says, 'the bones of the earth, its spine, like antelope's spine.' Ours, too, bone littering here – the cold, the Illness, the flint arrow, hand unseen. We pass quickly by.

Bone is hard. Hard beneath our feet, clad in deer-skin, skin soon shorn, worn away. Hard.

We keep on.

On, along the tops, where we can see. Where we should see the hand, the arrow, but don't.

On.

Then…

'Dig,' Old Man says. 'Here.' A cleft beside the track, where stone/bone breaks the surface, jagged, cragged, a bone hand reaching out.

We dig, stone to stone, scarp scraped, skin, flesh scraped to …bone (again)… our own, this time. Blood, flesh added to bone.

We keep on digging.

Sky-stone, this, colour same. Old Man wants something of the freed rocks. What? A circle? A god? Yes. We make a circle. And… what?

Old Man dies. We dig, again, a scoop in the earth, lay him down, lay stones down, hand-ful, this time, each of us, all of us, covering, up, up, skyward from the track, the spine. Stone, upon stone, upon stone.

Goodbye, Old Man.

We walk on.

Gold/Aur

She thinks they are talking of the sun, when they say they are walking to gold.

What else can it be – the sky's golden wheel, spokes of yellow beaming from it; gilding the land when it sets.

Where it sets is where they walk to; rising behind them, they, rising with it, then following, until it disappears ahead… somewhere. Always ahead. Will they ever reach it, she wonders?

Do they worship it, she wonders?

Straight, they go. Straight as their backs, as they march. Straight as their spears, held upright as they walk. Straight as their gaze, fixed on that sun… their gold.

Feet, boots, stamping up, down… hard down, pressing. Straightening the path as they go, lowering its surface, laying down stones to ease their strides – stones they find along the way, placed as if meaning something. (And yes, they meant something to her people, once, but what it is, she cannot remember).

They march, she follows. She is a camp-follower, after all, one of many – seeing to the soldiers' needs, whatever they may be; picked up as they go, like the stones.

He laughs – the one she 'serves' – when she tells him about the sun.

'No,' he says. 'This,' he says, pointing at the brooch that fastens his cloak, the eagle adorning their standard. 'We are walking to the shore, where we will cross the sea, and on to the mountains in that other land… where there is gold to be found… precious gold.'

'This is our golden road!' he says. 'If you serve me well, perhaps I will give you a coin, when I return!'

81

Now, as she walks, she scrapes the surface with her toe, keeps her head down, looking, searching. For what? A grain? A coin? A nugget? Dropped by those who came before? A small, hard thing. Dull.

She looks up at the sun again. Gold…

God/Duw

I am walking to God. So the holy men say. I am walking to the holy place, cradled in a vale, not far from the sea – the place where our Patron Saint was born and lived. If I reach there and return home, then come this way a second time, and a third, it shall be the same as a visit to Jerusalem. And I will be deemed holy enough to enter heaven. Thus… I am walking to God.

It is a strange path to take, along the ridge of these hills. And it is not a pleasant journey, stony in some parts, where my feet jar, muddy in others, where they sink down, to suck, slurp back up.

But it was never said that the road to the Lord would be easy.

And I have company. There are many pilgrims here, travelling the same way. All of us doing what pilgrims do – rise at dawn, pack, pray. Follow… follow whoever leads. There is always a leader, always a man, as Jesus was, as God is, as the Saint was. It is how it is.

… walking one step after another, in rain, wind (there is so much wind up here, rain, too). Heads down, pain reaching up from ground, through feet, legs, further; the cold creeping with it, to meet the cold from the air. Our bodies wanting to sink into the mud (where there is mud), to be cossetted, to sleep. Our bellies wanting fulness, our mouths dreaming of water.

On, on.

Thank you, Lord!

Cattle/Gwartheg

The noise travels along the path, first, it is said. On the mountains, there is the sough of the wind, the mew of the buzzard, the caw of the ravens – not much more, until we come along. Now, there is the lowing of the beasts, their shod hooves clipping the stones, gulping the mud. And the dogs, their barking, their whining, as they nip the heels above the hoof. And the sheep, and the geese, which may also follow.

But the noise of the men overwhelms all this – a song, almost, led by those in front... sounded in the back of the throat, no words to be spelled out and put on paper; an incessant whooping.

It warns of our coming.

It warns of the black beasts passing.

Of their bucking, thundering, wheeling, churning. The stench, the filth (the ordure, the urine), the blood, the carcasses of those who fall along the way... the way that widens, deepens, flattens with each journey to England... and back. Those who come back. Not all.

The Golden Road/Y Ffordd Aur

Whose footsteps do you walk in? If you stop, you will feel their passing, beneath your feet – on the path they made.

My Home in the Falls
Maddie Price

Ricketts Glen, a hike beyond
the thicket, with trails slick with
water drops. Stone steps seem to go
on eternally as the waves cascade from
the mountains, stone fountains, on the sharp
stalagmites below. So many feet have hiked here,
human feet amongst fossils, the trees new and green
like the Appalachian dream. Fall with it, the falls, jump
from its lip, the jagged cliffs, and find footing on the maple
roots. Tread lithe like the fauna in the misty woods and drink
in the rain forever running from above. And, welcome back home.

A Good Day
Eabhan Ní Shuileabháin

We went to the beach
Today, walked its shoreline,
The wind howling, freezing;
Three choughs flew and bickered,
And oystercatchers called –
We found mermaids' purses,
Empty small yellow shells and
A perfect stone heart.
Osian found silver –
A helium number three
He took from the wind.
We were woken
For a brief two hours
As we wound our way through sand
Under a wide sky
Where early sunset
Reflected all the fiery
Silver cloud linings.
Back home,
Osian made yellow star cards
And a maple cake;
You fixed the telescope,
Found Saturn almost
Touching Jupiter.

Cadover Bridge
Jonah Corren

After the climb, we gave a wide berth
to a nonplussed loiter of Belted Galloway,

and then headed through the centre of the next field,
towards the open moor. Tracking the left

of a dry-stone wall, fenced grazing blocked
the way between us and the thumbprint

of your car, nestled amongst a herd of others
by the side of the road. So, instead, we rounded

the crest of the hillside, surfers
navigating the inside curl of the wave,

and followed it down to its trough:
the dumpy and weather-beaten Cadover Cross.

Propped upright in its stone socket, the monks of
the Plympton Priory used it to mark the route

to their parishes nearby. Piss-poor pilgrims we'd have made,
laboured breaths rupturing God's own silence.

At the car park, an ice-cream van
had set up shop in its far corner,

and an elderly couple sat in their baby-blue supermini,
latticed cones gripped. Even from outside, we could hear

the blare of a song I recognised, but couldn't place.
Tracing their gaze, I found myself back at

the footpath, the ridge of footprints, the smudges
of cows, and, for a moment, I could see the outline

where we had been, trudging flies on
a pane of frosted glass. I took your hand, brushed the cold

from your palm, and caught your eyes in the
late light. You were, I'm certain, thinking the same.

Safety Notices

Ros Woolner

When I walk around the pond
these November afternoons,
hood up, hands in pockets,
I don't stray off the tarmacked path,
push through bulrushes
and enter the brown water.
I leave reflected houses undisturbed.
And I keep out of the wilderness
on the other side of the fence.
I don't climb iron railings,
drop down onto rough grass,
wander up the slope and onto the tracks
where trains speed past
to Manchester and Birmingham.
No, I keep my eyes on the yellow
birches and I stick to the path.

About Arachne Press

Arachne Press is a micro publisher of (award-winning!) short story and poetry anthologies and collections, novels including a Carnegie Medal nominated young adult novel, and a photographic portrait collection.

We are expanding our range all the time, but the short form is our first love. We keep fiction and poetry live, through readings, festivals (in particular our Solstice Shorts Festival), workshops, exhibitions and all things to do with writing.

https://arachnepress.com/

Follow us on Twitter:
@ArachnePress
@SolShorts

and Instagram
@ArachnePress

Like us on Facebook:
@ArachnePress
@SolsticeShorts2014

Find out more about our authors at
https://arachnepress.com/writers/